curious about

FIGURE SKATING

BY KRISSY EBERTH

AMICUS LEARNING

What are you

curious about?

CHAPTER THREE

Testing and Competing

Curious About is published
by Amcius Learning,
an imprint of Amicus
P.O. Box 227
Mankato, MN 56002
www.amicuspublishing.us

Editors: Grace Cain and Rebecca Glaser
Series Designer: Kathleen Petelinsek
Book Designer and Photo Researcher: Emily Dietz

Names: Eberth, Kristin, author.
Title: Curious about figure skating / by Krissy Eberth.
Description: Mankato, MN : Amicus Learning, 2025. | Series: Curious about sports | Includes bibliographical references and index. | Audience: Ages 5–9 | Audience: Grades 2-3 | Summary: "Conversational questions and answers share what kids can expect when they join figure skating, including what gear to bring, basic jumps and spins, and skating competitions. A Stay Curious! feature models research skills while simple infographics support visual literacy. Includes glossary and index"—Provided by publisher.
Identifiers: LCCN 2023043282 (print) | LCCN 2023043283 (ebook) | ISBN 9781645497097 (library binding) | ISBN 9781681529721 (paperback) | ISBN 9781645497158 (ebook)
Subjects: LCSH: Figure skating–Juvenile literature.
Classification: LCC GV850.4 .E34 2025 (print) | LCC GV850.4 (ebook) | DDC 796.91/2-dc23/eng/20230929
LC record available at https://lccn.loc.gov/2023043282
LC ebook record available at https://lccn.loc.gov/2023043283

Photo Credits: Alamy/Buddy Mays, 13; Dreamstime/Volha Yarmolenka, 3, 21; Freep!k/seventyfour, 10–11; Getty/Catherine Ivill, 19, Joosep Martinson, 15; iStock/bgblue, 22, 23, bortonia, 22, 23, Brightrock, 20, JulPo, 7, Liudmila Chernetska, 2, 8, noblige, 5, RichLegg, 9, SeventyFour, 2, 9, 12, simonkr, 16–17, Ulza, 6; Shutterstock/Aija Lehtonen, 15, Iurii Osadchi, 14, Master1305, Cover, 1, Nadezhda Tulatova, 9, Olga Besnard, 15

Printed in China

CHAPTER ONE

How do I learn to figure skate?

Find an ice rink and sign up for a class. You will start in group lessons. Your coach will teach you to march on the ice. Keep your arms out for balance. Then you'll learn to glide, stop, and turn. After you can do the basics, you can take higher classes.

Don't have skates? Don't worry. You can rent ice skates at many rinks.

How old do I need to be to figure skate?

Learning to skate is more fun with a friend.

Any age! Most clubs offer classes for ages three and up. Many skaters start around age five or six. Boys and girls can both figure skate. Even adults can learn. Some skaters learn for fun. Other skaters take tests and compete.

What gear do I need?

Figure skates have toe picks on the blade. They help a skater do difficult skills like jumps and spins.

You'll need ice skates. Make sure they fit right. If they are too big, you might trip. If they are too small, they will hurt your feet. Skate guards will protect your blades off the ice. Wear snug but stretchy clothing. This will help you move easily. Some beginners skate with a helmet, too.

Snug clothing and gloves will keep you warm on the cold rink.

SKATE GUARDS

HARD GUARDS

- Protect your blades when you walk off ice.
- TIP: Don't leave hard guards on when your skates are wet. The blades will rust.

SOFT GUARDS

- Protect your blades when you put them in a bag.
- TIP: Wipe off your blades with a towel after skating.

CHAPTER TWO

Where do I practice?

At an ice rink! Many indoor rinks are open all year. Join a skating club so you can practice with other figure skaters. You can train off the ice, too. Stretching and working out helps skaters gain strength. It takes a lot of practice to master difficult moves.

Learning to balance on one foot while skating takes practice.

A private coach will work with more advanced skaters.

Who is my coach?

Someone who has skated a lot! A teenager in your club may coach young skaters. Most coaches are professionals. As you learn more, you can get a private coach. They will teach you harder jumps and spins. They will create a **program** for you if you want to compete.

A skating coach teaches group lessons for beginners.

When can I start jumping and spinning?

First, make sure you know the basics. You'll practice these over and over. This builds muscle memory and **coordination**. Your coach will know when you're ready to learn new skills. You will start with a **waltz jump** and two-foot spin. These are building blocks to harder skills.

TYPES OF FIGURE SKATING

Singles

Jumps and spins take a lot of practice!

Pairs

Ice Dance

Synchronized

CHAPTER THREE

What is a figure skating competition like?

There are music, costumes, and judges. You will compete against other skaters at your level. Girls usually wear a skating dress. Boys wear pants and a shirt. A group of judges will watch you skate and give you a score. The person with the highest score wins!

At a competition, skaters wear fancy costumes. They often skate to music.

How do I move up to higher levels?

You take a test! Each level has harder skills. Your coach will help you get ready for testing. In a test, a group of judges watches your skills or your program. They decide if you pass. It's exciting to move up a level!

DID YOU KNOW?

Some figure skaters learn different programs for competitions, tests, and shows. That's a lot to remember!

Skating in front of a judge lets you show what you've learned.

What else can I do besides competing?

Performing at an ice show is a fun part of skating.

Many clubs have a show or **recital**. It is held at the end of the season. Skaters may perform in small groups or large groups. Some clubs do shows with characters and tell a story. This is a great way to celebrate your hard work!

DID YOU KNOW?
Some figure skaters don't jump at all! They ice dance. They are judged on their footwork, lifts, and spins.

Two young skaters perform an ice dance program.

STAY CURIOUS!

ASK MORE QUESTIONS

What's the highest test level?

How do I know if I skate right-handed or left-handed?

Try a BIG QUESTION: Is figure skating easier or harder than other sports?

SEARCH FOR ANSWERS

Search the library catalog or the Internet.
A librarian, teacher, or parent can help you.

Using Keywords
Find the looking glass.

Keywords are the most important words in your question.

If you want to know about:

- the highest test level, type: FIGURE SKATING HIGHEST LEVEL
- which way to skate, type: FIGURE SKATING HANDEDNESS

LEARN MORE

FIND GOOD SOURCES

Here are some good, safe sources you can use in your research.
Your librarian can help you find more.

Books

Figure Skating
by Ashley Gish, 2022.

Figure Skating
by Julie Murray, 2023.

Who is Nathan Chen?
by Joseph Liu, 2023.

Internet Sites

Britannica Kids | Ice Skating
https://kids.britannica.com/kids/article/ice-skating/437405
This site provides history of ice skating as an activity and sport, as well as fun facts.

Kiddle | Figure Skating
https://kids.kiddle.co/Figure_skating
This site provides a child-friendly explanation of the moves, rules, and judging of figure skating.

Every effort has been made to ensure that these websites are appropriate for children. However, because of the nature of the Internet, it is impossible to guarantee that these sites will remain active indefinitely or that their contents will not be altered.

SHARE AND TAKE ACTION

Join a beginner class.
Ask a friend to go with you.

Go to a figure skating recital or competition.
Watch as the figure skaters do different jumps and spins.

Choose a song and make up your own program.
Head outside with a friend and perform the routine on the grass.

GLOSSARY

coordination The ability to move different parts of your body together well or easily.

ice dance A type of skating where a team of two perform moves that look like ballroom dancing on ice.

program A performance set to music that shows a skater's skills through a number of planned moves that flow together in a graceful sequence.

recital A dance or musical performance given by a single skater or a group of skaters.

waltz jump A forward half rotation that starts by taking off on one foot and landing on the other foot.

INDEX

About the Author

Krissy Eberth is a former professional figure skater and a United States Figure Skating double gold medalist. When away from her writing desk, she can be found skiing, hiking, or biking the trails of northern Minnesota.